A STUDIO PRESS BOOK

First published in the UK in 2020 by Studio Press Books,
an imprint of Bonnier Books UK,
The Plaza, 535 King's Road,
London, SW10 0SZ
Owned by Bonnier Books,
Sveavägen 56, Stockholm, Sweden

studiopressbooks.co.uk
bonnierbooks.co.uk
beano.com

A Beano Studios Product © DC Thomson (2020)

Printed in Poland
3 5 7 9 10 8 6 4

All rights reserved
ISBN 978-17874-1-705-2

Written by Rachel Elliot
Edited by Stephanie Milton
Designed by Hannah Baldwin and Rob Ward

MIX
Paper from
responsible sources
FSC® C018236
FSC
www.fsc.org

CONTENTS

VISITORS' GUIDE

WELCOME TO OUR TOWN!

Beanotown is a great place for anyone who loves catapults, pranks and peashooters, and wants to hang out in a place where kids rule. This visitors' guide will help you to explore the real Beanotown, stay alert for mischief-makers and bamboozle your enemies – just like a true Beanotown resident.

Super-secret tunnels, dens, treehouses and bags of mayhem are waiting for you in the heart of this prank-tastic place. Come and join in the fun!

"VIKINGS BUILT THE ORIGINAL BEANOTOWN. TO FIND OUT MORE ABOUT ITS AWESOME HISTORY, TURN TO PAGES 60-61."

4

1	8:45 To Mars	4	Bash Street School	7	Beanoland Theme Park
2	Mount Beano	5	Beanotown Woods	8	Bunkerton Castle
3	Cold Trafford	6	The Menace House	9	Beanotown Lighthouse

HOW TO GET HERE
(AND HOW TO LEAVE)

TRAINS

Beanotown Railway Station is at the very end of the line. Train drivers screech to a halt here and leave faster than Billy Whizz in a hurry to get home for their dinner, so don't dawdle! Oh, and if you see Dennis and Gnasher on the platform, take our advice: choose their carriage.

BUSES

Beanotown's red double deckers are a great way to get to know the town: while you're waiting at the bus stop, you're sure to see plenty of mischief. When the bus arrives, carefully check your seat before you sit down. You never know what you might find…

BEANOTOWN BUS BINGO

It's fun to play bus bingo in Beanotown. When you have found everything in a horizontal line, pop into the Beanotown Bus Station while you're here and we'll present you with your prize – a bag of hand sanitiser, a scrubbing brush and a bottle of bus cleaner.

DEAD FLIES	HARD CHEWING GUM	SMELLY SOCK	SWEET WRAPPER	WATER BALLOON
PEA SHOOTER	CUSTARD PIE	CAN OF WORMS	MOULDY CHEESE	SANDWICH CRUSTS
EAR WAX	SPLAT OF TOMATO SAUCE	CATAPULT	FLUFF-COVERED STICKY SWEET	ITCHING POWDER
SOMEONE'S HOMEWORK	BISCUIT CRUMBS	STINK BOMB	OLD COPY OF THE BEANO	FISH BONES
SECRET MESSAGE	SOGGY SPROUT	BEANOTOWN BURGERS WRAPPER	SQUISHY TOMATO	WHOOPEE CUSHION

WEIRD WAYS TO TRAVEL

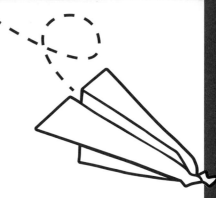

8:45 TO MARS

Even Beanotown's finest sometimes need a quick getaway. The 8:45 to Mars zips between Beanotown and outer space for the price of a fake pimple.

LORD SNOOTY'S AIR BALLOON

If you get really stuck, you could always ask Lord Snooty for a ride in his fabulous air balloon. You'll find him at Bunkerton Castle, if the drawbridge is down.

HOW TO COMPLETELY ESCAPE

If your pranks are catching up with you and you need to leave town in a hurry, head over to the clock tower on top of the town hall. (Watch out for the Mayor – he'd love to get his hands on this mind-blowing secret.) Only Dennis and Gnasher know what's really inside. Someone properly awesome told Dennis about it – himself!

Future Dennis travelled back in time to tell himself that the clock tower is the home of the world's one and only time machine. It is strictly for naughty pranks and mischief-making. Anyone caught using the time machine for boring history lessons will have to spend five minutes alone with Dennis and the entire contents of the Beanotown joke shop. Using it to escape is allowed, so jump in and bash stuff until something happens. (There are instructions somewhere, but Dennis has never read them, so it's no use asking him.) Happy travels!

HOW TO FIND YOUR WAY AROUND

Beanotown's brick houses are brightened up with colourful front doors, garish shops and regular rotten tomato splats. Where else would you find 'no catapult' signs, prank warnings and a library with a slide inside? The trouble is, it can be a bit confusing for new visitors, so here's a handy guide to what some of the signs mean and what to do when you see them.

HEAD STRAIGHT TO NUMBER 51 TO PICK UP SOME PRANKING TIPS FROM DENNIS MENACE.

GASWORKS ROAD

WARNING: PARENTS WHO LEAVE CHILDREN UNATTENDED WILL BE SPLATTED

BEANOTOWN SHOPS AND CAFES ARE WELL PREPARED FOR SOLO PRANKSTERS. ALL UNACCOMPANIED KIDS ARE GIVEN A CATAPULT AND A BUCKET OF ROTTEN TOMATOES, AND TOLD TO FIND THEIR PARENTS.

DO NOT PRESS THIS BUTTON. NO MATTER WHAT. JUST DON'T.

RUN FASTER.

RUN.

PRESS THIS BUTTON FOR A SURPRISE!

IGNORE THIS SIGN. PRANKSTERS ON SKATEBOARDS MAY CRASH INTO YOU FROM ANY DIRECTION.

ONE WAY

9

THE MENACE FAMILY

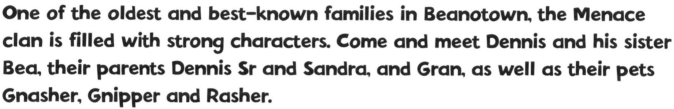

One of the oldest and best-known families in Beanotown, the Menace clan is filled with strong characters. Come and meet Dennis and his sister Bea, their parents Dennis Sr and Sandra, and Gran, as well as their pets Gnasher, Gnipper and Rasher.

DENNIS MENACE

Dennis Menace, the terror of Beanotown and the world's wildest boy, is smart, fun, adventurous and always on speaking terms with trouble. He's constantly on the lookout for laughs and enjoys coming up with fun pranks.

His teachers don't understand how clever he is, because his brain doesn't get fired up by sums and spellings. Instead, he loves exploring. For instance, once he explored what would make the biggest splash in the Beanotown pond. (The answer? Sergeant Slipper.) Another time he explored what would happen if he filled a balloon with custard. It's just curiosity! But somehow, teachers don't see the same exciting possibilities as Dennis.

Walter Brown is the opposite of Dennis and exists to challenge him at every turn, usually by spoiling his adventures. Luckily, Dennis has plenty of friends who love life as much as he does. His best friend is Gnasher the dog, who shares all Dennis's secrets. He's also great mates with Roger the Dodger, Pieface, Rubi, JJ and Minnie the Minx. If you make friends with Dennis while you're visiting Beanotown, be prepared for anything. You're in for a crazy ride!

WALTER BROWN

"I WONDER WHAT WOULD HAPPEN IF..."

Dennis's treehouse is filled with everything a prankster could possibly need. If you're lucky enough to get invited in, make sure you check out the comic collection, practise with some of Dennis's awesome catapults and steer well clear of the stinky socks…

FACT FILE
BIRTHDAY: 17TH MARCH
ADDRESS: 51 GASWORKS ROAD
SCHOOL: BASH STREET SCHOOL, CLASS 3C
LIKES: COMPUTER GAMES, MISCHIEF, MAYHEM, SKATEBOARDING, PLAYING GUITAR
DISLIKES: HOMEWORK
BIGGEST FEAR: DENNIS HAS NO FEAR!
BEST QUALITY: BRAVERY
TOP SKILLS: MISCHIEF-MAKING, SKATEBOARDING
FAVOURITE FOOD: BEANOTOWN BURGERS

BEA MENACE

Dennis's little sister is only one year old, but she already has her own set of top pranks and tricks. Known as the human stink-bomb, she can fill her nappy on demand and produce some totally unbelievable whiffs. She can also turn a plate of food into a weapon, aimed and fired in seconds.

Bea adores Dennis, especially when he invents super-exciting bedtime stories for her – fairy tales with a twist of mischief. She's fond of Gnipper, who puts up with her bashing him with her rattle in return for being allowed to steal her toys.

FACT FILE

BIRTHDAY: 8TH AUGUST
ADDRESS: 51 GASWORKS ROAD
LIKES: BASHING THINGS, FINGER PAINTING
DISLIKES: DENNIS'S ENEMIES
BIGGEST FEAR: LOSING HER TEDDY
BEST QUALITY: CUTENESS
TOP SKILLS: NAPPY FILLING, FARTING, FOOD THROWING, EMBARRASSING HER PARENTS
FAVOURITE FOOD: MUSH

WHERE TO FIND BEA

YOU MIGHT SEE BEA CRAWLING TOWARDS TROUBLE, OR EVEN TODDLING TOWARDS IT IF IT'S SOMETHING REALLY COOL. IF SHE'S HEADING IN YOUR DIRECTION, TRY TO STAY OUT OF THE LINE OF FIRE.

"ME CAN DO THAT!"

DID YOU KNOW?
Bea is short for Beatrice.

"GNASH!"   "GNASH!"

GNASHER

This Abyssinian wire-haired tripe hound was found by Dennis Menace when he was a stray puppy, and they've been the best of friends ever since. Gnasher is more than a match for any enemy. He has incredibly powerful jaw muscles, concrete-smashingly strong teeth, and a coat as rough as barbed wire.

Gnasher carries a family of fleas in his coat, and they are just as gnaughty as Gnasher himself. He's also super fast and can easily keep up with Dennis on his bike or skateboard.

Even though he is best friends with Dennis, he doesn't always agree with him. However, he shares Dennis's love of mischief, and Dennis has no idea how wise his four-legged friend really is.

DID YOU KNOW?
Gnasher's other children are called Gnancy, Gnatasha, Gnaomi, Gnanette and Gnorah.

FACT FILE
DATE OF BIRTH: 31ST AUGUST
ADDRESS: 51 GASWORKS ROAD
LIKES: DENNIS, EATING, MISCHIEF, SCRATCHING
DISLIKES: FANCY DRESS, WALTER BROWN
BIGGEST FEAR: GOING TO THE VET, BATHTIME
BEST QUALITY: LOYALTY
TOP SKILLS: GNASHING THINGS WITH HIS SUPER-STRONG JAWS, CHASING THE POSTMAN
FAVOURITE FOOD: SAUSAGES

WHERE TO FIND GNASHER
WHEN HE'S NOT CAUSING MAYHEM WITH DENNIS, GNASHER CAN USUALLY BE FOUND IN HIS SUPER-COOL KENNEL. IT HAS EVERYTHING A FOUR-LEGGED PRANKSTER COULD WANT, FROM THE LIVE POSTIE-CAM TO THE CAT THUMPER AND THE SAUSAGE-MAKING MACHINE.

13

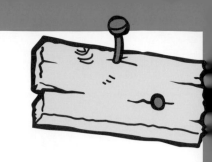

DENNIS MENACE SR

When he was a kid (back when dinosaurs ruled the earth) Dennis's dad loved pranks just as much as Dennis. Tragically, he had to grow up, and being an adult made him forget how much fun he used to have. Now he spends most of his time worrying about money.

Dennis Sr loves spending time in his shed, where he can escape the neighbours complaining about Dennis and demanding money to mend the things he's broken.

DID YOU KNOW?
Dennis Sr is scared of swans.

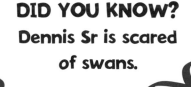
"HOW MUCH IS THIS GOING TO COST?"

FACT FILE
BIRTHDAY: 17TH MARCH (JUST LIKE DENNIS)
ADDRESS: 51 GASWORKS ROAD
JOB: QUALITY CONTROL SUPERVISOR AT PERKINS' PAPERCLIP FACTORY
LIKES: GETTING A BIT OF PEACE IN HIS SHED, SAVING MONEY
DISLIKES: MOWING THE LAWN, WILBUR BROWN
BIGGEST FEAR: WHAT DENNIS IS GOING TO DO NEXT
BEST QUALITY: STICKS UP FOR DENNIS
TOP SKILLS: BODGED DIY TO SAVE MONEY, ABILITY TO SLEEP ANYWHERE
FAVOURITE FOOD: PIZZA

SANDRA MENACE

Dennis's mum is clever, firm and well-organised. She loves her family, and puts her foot down firmly when necessary. Sandra is good at understanding people and knows how to stay calm no matter what happens.

Sandra's best friend is her sister, Vicky Makepeace, who is also Minnie the Minx's mum.

"LIFE'S WHAT YOU MAKE IT."

DID YOU KNOW?
Sandra has a secret career as a ninja who borrows from the rich to help those who don't have so much. Her secret cupboard is a treasure trove of awesome equipment.

FACT FILE
BIRTHDAY: 19TH MAY
ADDRESS: 51 GASWORKS ROAD
JOB: PERSONAL ASSISTANT TO WILBUR BROWN, THE MAYOR OF BEANOTOWN
LIKES: FAMILY TIME, HIGH CRIME, ART
DISLIKES: MISCHIEVOUS BEHAVIOUR
BIGGEST FEAR: HER FAMILY BEING HURT
BEST QUALITY: BEING FAIR AND TOLERANT
TOP SKILLS: IMAGINATIVE, HARD-WORKING, ORGANISED
FAVOURITE FOOD: ITALIAN

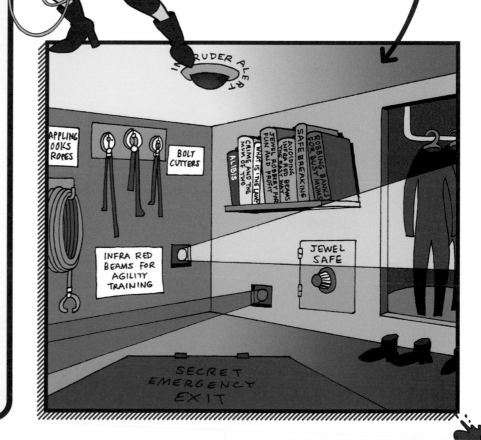

"CHILL OUT!"

GRAN MENACE

Dennis's gran is his dad's mum, and she remembers all the antics Dennis Sr used to get up to when he was a boy. She's very wise and she never judges Dennis. She understands how important it is for kids to have fun all the time, and thinks that grown-ups should just chill out.

DID YOU KNOW?
Gran is 70 years old and her name is Catherine.

FACT FILE

BIRTHDAY: 23RD AUGUST
ADDRESS: 67 SUTHERLAND CRESCENT
JOB: RETIRED
LIKES: HAVING FUN, SEEING HER GRANDCHILDREN, RIDING HER MOTORBIKE
DISLIKES: TAKING LIFE TOO SERIOUSLY
BIGGEST FEAR: THE GAS BILL
BEST QUALITY: WISDOM
TOP SKILLS: MOTORBIKE RIDING, SIDING WITH DENNIS
FAVOURITE FOOD: BISCUITS

GNIPPER

"GNIP!"

Gnipper has the same powerful teeth and rough coat as his father, Gnasher, but he still has a lot to learn. He loves spending time with Gnasher and Dennis, but he is Bea's puppy and they share the same sense of humour.

DID YOU KNOW?
Gnasher and Gnipper can understand each other, but no one else knows what they are saying.

RASHER

Mr and Mrs Menace couldn't face looking after a pet pig as well as a pet tripe hound, but Gran knew that Dennis would be miserable without Rasher. She gave the porker a home, and now Dennis can visit whenever he likes. Rasher two favourite things are making a mess and eating turnips.

"GRUNT!"

DID YOU KNOW?
Rasher collects turnips.

17

DENNIS'S MOST IMPRESSIVE PRANKS

Everyone in Beanotown knows that Dennis is the prince of pranks. Which ones have been the most successful? Watch out for these tricks during your visit to Beanotown.

MIXED ITCHING POWDER WITH THE LAUNDRY.

FROZE HIS DAD'S BOWL OF CEREAL.

STUCK GOOGLY EYES ON ALL THE EGGS.

REPLACED THE TOMATO SAUCE WITH STRAWBERRY JAM.

PRANKED EVERYONE BY NOT PRANKING THEM — HE MADE EVERYONE VERY ANXIOUS TRYING TO GUESS WHAT HE WAS GOING TO DO NEXT!

FILLED THE BATHROOM SOAP DISPENSER WITH MAPLE SYRUP.

PAPERCLIPPED ALL BEA'S NAPPIES TOGETHER.

PUT HAIR DYE IN A BOTTLE OF MRS CREECHER'S SHAMPOO.

HID A TRICK SPIDER IN HIS DAD'S PANTS DRAWER.

SQUEEZED A RUBBER SNAKE INTO THE CUTLERY DRAWER.

HID ALL THE PENS IN BASH STREET SCHOOL.

MINNIE'S MOST MAGNIFICENT MINXES

Dennis's cousin Minnie has a knack for thinking up the most devastating and destructive minxes, so don't be fooled by the innocent expressions she practises in the mirror.

SWAPPED HER DAD'S TOOTHPASTE WITH A TUBE OF SUPERDUPERGLUE.

SHOUTED 'BOO!' OVER THE SUPERMARKET SPEAKER SYSTEM.

DROPPED A BOX OF STINK BOMBS IN THE LOCAL JOKE SHOP. OOPS!

STRETCHED CLING FILM OVER HER BEDROOM DOORWAY TO KEEP EVERYONE OUT.

DRESSED UP AS A ZOMBIE TO SCARE OFF UNWANTED VISITORS.

HID FIVE ALARM CLOCKS IN HER PARENT'S BEDROOM, ALL SET FOR 2AM.

WRAPPED HER ENTIRE HOUSE IN TOILET PAPER.

GLUED WALTER'S POCKET MONEY TO THE PAVEMENT.

PUT CREEPY CRAWLIES IN ALL THE MATCHBOXES.

FED HER FAMILY'S LAUNDRY TO A HERD OF HUNGRY GOATS.

DRESSED ALL THE SNOWMEN IN BEANOTOWN IN RED STRIPY TOPS AND MINNIE-STYLE BLACK BERETS.

CHANGED ALL THE CLOCKS SO HER MUM AND DAD MISSED PARENTS' EVENING.

THE MAKEPEACE FAMILY

The Makepeace family is well known in Beanotown, and Minnie is as infamous as her cousin Dennis. She lives with her parents, Vicky and Darren, and her cat Chester. Her five older brothers, Michael, Martin, Mark, Morris and Max, have all left home.

MINNIE THE MINX

DID YOU KNOW?
Minnie's real name is Hermione.

As the youngest child in a big family, Minnie is a dab hand at getting attention. Her fearless, enthusiastic attitude sometimes leads her into trouble, but she's a quick thinker and acts fast, making things up as she goes along.

Minnie doesn't care about being liked, but she wants to be respected. As far as she's concerned, she's tougher, smarter and better looking than anyone else. She likes facts and logic, but blathering on about feelings is a waste of good minxing time.

Minnie is great at solving problems, and loves learning – when she can see that there's a point. Sadly, what Mrs Creecher wants her to learn at Bash Street School is totally and utterly pointless. Minnie's a natural leader who is full of fun ideas. Somehow, people find themselves doing what she wants!

UNSCRAMBLE THESE LETTERS TO DISCOVER ONE OF MINNIE'S FAVOURITE WORDS.

INTOCA

ACTION

THE DARK MINX

One of Beanotown's greatest secrets is the fact that Minnie has another identity. When she dons her mask and cape, she becomes the Dark Minx – a shadowy superhero who plagues the town in the name of justice.

WHERE TO FIND MINNIE

MINNIE IS ALWAYS BUSY. YOU MIGHT SPOT HER SETTING UP A PRANK WITH DENNIS AND ROGER, BURSTING THROUGH A SKYLIGHT AS THE DARK MINX, OR ATTEMPTING TO TUNNEL OUT OF BASH STREET SCHOOL. THE BEST WAY TO FIND MINNIE IS TO STAY STILL AND LISTEN FOR THE YELLS!

FACT FILE

BIRTHDAY: 19TH DECEMBER
ADDRESS:
54 GASWORKS ROAD
SCHOOL: BASH STREET
SCHOOL, CLASS 3C
LIKES: READING, ACTION,
DRAWING COMICS
DISLIKES: PLANNING,
PUSSY-FOOTING AROUND
BIGGEST FEAR: PEOPLE
THINKING SHE'S WEAK
BEST QUALITY: LOYALTY,
BRAVERY, INTELLIGENCE
TOP SKILLS: PEASHOOTER
USE, FACE PULLING,
FOOTBALL
FAVOURITE FOOD: PIZZA

"GET ON WITH IT!"

MINNIE'S BEDROOM

VICKY MAKEPEACE

Minnie's mum is a kind and enthusiastic person who loves people and likes to get involved in as many clubs and activities as possible. She loves her daughter just the way she is, and admires her determination to get what she wants out of life.

Vicky is good friends with her little sister, Sandra Menace. They live on the same street and often pop round to each other's house for chats.

FACT FILE

BIRTHDAY: 23RD DECEMBER
ADDRESS: 54 GASWORKS ROAD
JOB: HR MANAGER AT PERKINS' PAPERCLIP FACTORY
LIKES: HAVING LOTS OF CLUBS AND HOBBIES
DISLIKES: HAVING NOTHING TO DO
BIGGEST FEAR: MICE
BEST QUALITY: ENTHUSIASM, PATIENCE
TOP SKILLS: ORGANISATION, PEOPLE MANAGEMENT
FAVOURITE FOOD: CHINESE

DID YOU KNOW?
Vicky has been married to Darren for 24 years.

CHESTER THE CAT

Chester is very independent and knows exactly what he wants – and what he doesn't want. Usually, what he doesn't want is to get mixed up in Minnie's crazy schemes, and yet somehow it keeps happening.

Chester would love to spend his time sleeping in a cosy corner, but chilling out is always unlikely while Minnie's around. Instead, he is often found minxing with his mistress – and sometimes ending up the victim.

DID YOU KNOW?
CHESTER SOMETIMES GETS INTO MISCHIEF OF HIS OWN WITH DODGE CAT AND WINSTON.

"MEOW!"

DARREN MAKEPEACE

If you need advice about money while you're in Beanotown, head over to the Makepeace family home. Darren is great with numbers – he has had to be with six children to bring up! He loves Minnie, but he wishes that she would be more interested in cuddly toys, good manners and fairy stories, and less interested in peashooters, pranks and mayhem.

In his spare time, Darren likes reading newspapers and making models from matchsticks.

"BE PREPARED."

DID YOU KNOW?
Darren is a black belt in judo.

FACT FILE

BIRTHDAY: 14TH OCTOBER
ADDRESS: 54 GASWORKS ROAD
JOB: ACCOUNTANT FOR THE SCRIMP CORPORATION
LIKES: PLANNING, FACTS, MODEL-MAKING, SUMS
DISLIKES: SURPRISES, ART, UNPREDICTABILITY
BIGGEST FEAR: TAKING RISKS
BEST QUALITY: STAYING CALM IN A CRISIS
TOP SKILLS: MANAGING MONEY
FAVOURITE FOOD: FISH AND CHIPS

THE BASH STREET KIDS

The ten members of Class 2B are known as the Bash Street Kids: Danny, Smiffy, Fatty, Cuthbert, Sidney, Toots, Spotty, Wilfrid, Plug and 'Erbert. They argue with each other all the time, but woe betide any newcomers who criticise them. The Bash Street Kids are a tight-knit bunch.

DANNY MORGAN

Danny is the leader of the Bash Street Kids, and he can be trusted to provide lots and lots of fun. For a clue to his character, just check out his skull-and-crossbones jersey. He's a rule-breaking pirate, and you cross him at your peril.

"A PIRATE'S LIFE FOR ME!"

FACT FILE

AGE: 9
ADDRESS: EIGHTH FLOOR, BASH STREET TOWERS
SCHOOL: BASH STREET SCHOOL, CLASS 2B
BEST FRIEND: SIDNEY
WORST ENEMY: CUTHBERT
PRIZED POSSESSION: TELESCOPE
TOP SKILLS: COURAGE, LEADERSHIP
FAMILY: MUM AND OLDER BROTHER FRANK

DID YOU KNOW?
Danny's great-great-great grandparents were real pirates!

SMIFFY SMITH

Smiffy isn't exactly what you might call a brainbox (except in his own family). But you don't have to be clever to be a good friend, and Smiffy is super loyal. He's always ready to join in with Danny's madcap schemes, and occasionally his foolish statements turn out to be surprisingly wise.

Smiffy has a pet pebble called Kevin.

DID YOU KNOW?
Smiffy's real name is Aristotle. He's named after a famous Greek philosopher from over 2,000 years ago. (That's even older than your teacher.)

FACT FILE

AGE: 9
ADDRESS: THE BASEMENT, BASH STREET TOWERS
SCHOOL: BASH STREET SCHOOL, CLASS 2B
BEST FRIENDS: KEVIN THE PEBBLE, TOOTS AND THE BEANOTOWN LOLLIPOP LADY
WORST ENEMY: CARROTS
PRIZED POSSESSION: HIS COLLECTION OF USED RAFFLE TICKETS
TOP SKILLS: BREAKING IDIOT-PROOF DEVICES
FAMILY: MUM, DAD AND BROTHER NORMAN

"EVERYTHING IS SO DELICIOUS!"

FATTY BROWN

Fatty enjoys food and always scoffs everything on his plate – even the yucktacular school dinners. In fact, Dennis often passes his portions to Fatty. Like all the Bash Street Kids, Fatty is happy with himself just the way he is – especially his awesome gymnastics skills.

FACT FILE

AGE: 9
ADDRESS: 28 ACACIA ROAD
SCHOOL: BASH STREET SCHOOL, CLASS 2B
BEST FRIEND: 'ERBERT
WORST ENEMY: CUTHBERT
PRIZED POSSESSION: AN APRON SIGNED BY MARY BERRY
TOP SKILL: GYMNASTICS
FAMILY: MUM, DAD AND BABY SISTER FELICITY

CUTHBERT CRINGEWORTHY

Cuthbert is the only member of Class 2B who wears the uniform and does his homework. He's not a popular boy, but underneath all his swotty, tell-tale bluster, he's just nervous. The rest of Class 2B keep him safe from becoming too snobbish and devious. One Walter in the school is enough!

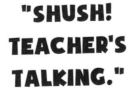

"SHUSH! TEACHER'S TALKING."

FACT FILE

AGE: 9
ADDRESS: 28A ACACIA ROAD
SCHOOL: BASH STREET SCHOOL, CLASS 2B
BEST FRIEND: TEACHER
WORST ENEMY: ANYONE WHO IS ANNOYING TEACHER
PRIZED POSSESSION: A FRAMED PHOTOGRAPH OF TEACHER
TOP SKILL: GETTING OTHER KIDS INTO TROUBLE FOR MISBEHAVING
FAMILY: MUM, DAD, PET KOI CARP

"FIRST THE WORST, SECOND THE BEST!"

Born a few minutes after his twin sister Toots, Sidney is a natural prankster with a great sense of humour and a fiery streak. He gets on well with most of the other kids in 2B and is a great team player. Sidney loves animals, and keeps his pets on the roof of Bash Street Towers.

FACT FILE

AGE: 9
ADDRESS: TOP FLOOR, BASH STREET TOWERS
SCHOOL: BASH STREET SCHOOL, CLASS 2B
BEST FRIEND: TOOTS
WORST ENEMY: ALSO TOOTS!
PRIZED POSSESSION: PATRICK, HIS PET PIGEON
TOP SKILL: MAKING FRIENDS WITH ANY ANIMAL
FAMILY: MUM, DAD AND TWIN SISTER TOOTS

TOOTS (SYDNEY KATE PYE)

Toots is the only girl in Class 2B, and the second in command after Danny. (Actually, she often has a strong opinion about his decisions.) She will always stand up for the underdog. When she and Sidney were born, their parents couldn't think of two different names, so they chose different spellings of the same name.

FACT FILE

AGE: 9
ADDRESS: TOP FLOOR, BASH STREET TOWERS
SCHOOL: BASH STREET SCHOOL, CLASS 2B
BEST FRIEND: SIDNEY
WORST ENEMY: ALSO SIDNEY!
PRIZED POSSESSION: HER BMX BIKE
TOP SKILL: PLAYING FOOTBALL, STREET DANCING
FAMILY: MUM, DAD AND TWIN BROTHER SIDNEY

"I'M IN CHARGE!"

"THE BEST FORM OF ATTACK IS ATTACK."

JAMES CAMERON (SPOTTY)

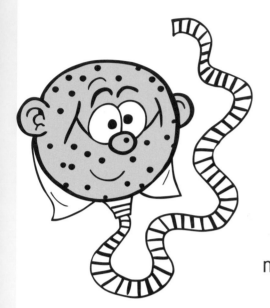

You'll recognise Spotty by his long, stripy tie, pimples and Scottish accent. He has a sarcastic sense of humour and can sometimes say things that sound a little bit cruel. The one person he never cheeks is Dennis.

FACT FILE

AGE: 9
ADDRESS: EIGHTH FLOOR, BASH STREET TOWERS
SCHOOL: BASH STREET SCHOOL, CLASS 2B
BEST FRIENDS: SIDNEY AND DANNY
WORST ENEMY: CUTHBERT
PRIZED POSSESSION: HIS SUPER-LONG SCHOOL TIE
TOP SKILL: STARTING ARGUMENTS
FAMILY: MUM, DAD AND BROTHER BRIAN

WILFRID WIMBLE

The shyest member of Class 2B also has a strong streak of mischief. He hides behind his jumper for comfort, and also to stop anyone from seeing the expression on his face. Adults assume that he's sweet and innocent, and he's very good at getting them to do what he wants.

FACT FILE

AGE: 9
ADDRESS: FIFTH FLOOR, BASH STREET TOWERS
SCHOOL: BASH STREET SCHOOL, CLASS 2B
BEST FRIEND: FATTY
WORST ENEMY: CUTHBERT
PRIZED POSSESSION: MAGIC TRICKS COLLECTION
TOP SKILL: DOING NIFTY MAGIC TRICKS, INCLUDING MAKING HIMSELF DISAPPEAR
FAMILY: DAD, ALFRED

"DON'T STICK YOUR NECK OUT."

"I'M SO HANDSOME."

PERCIVAL PROUDFOOT PLUGSLEY (PLUG)

Plug is sensitive and always thinks about how other people are feeling. He has no idea that other people think he's ugly, because he can see how beautiful he is on the inside, where it counts. That's how he looks at others too, so he is the first to notice their inner gorgeousness.

FACT FILE

AGE: 9
ADDRESS: 32 GASWORKS ROAD
SCHOOL: BASH STREET SCHOOL, CLASS 2B
BEST FRIENDS: WILFRID AND 'ERBERT
WORST ENEMY: GIRLS WHO START TO CRY WHEN THEY SEE HIS HANDSOME FACE – IT'S SO EMBARRASSING!
PRIZED POSSESSION: HIS AMAZING GOOD LOOKS
TOP SKILL: HE CAN SMASH A MIRROR BY WINKING AT IT
FAMILY: MUM AND DAD, WHO ARE JUST AS GORGEOUS AS PLUG

HERBERT HENRY HOOVER ('ERBERT)

FACT FILE

AGE: 9
ADDRESS: SECOND FLOOR, BASH STREET TOWERS
SCHOOL: BASH STREET SCHOOL, CLASS 2B
BEST FRIENDS: PLUG AND WILFRID
WORST ENEMY: CUTHBERT
PRIZED POSSESSION: GLASSES
TOP SKILL: USING HIS OTHER SENSES
FAMILY: MUM, DAD AND COUSIN HENRIETTA

"WHERE DID HE GO?"

'Erbert is known for being very short-sighted, but he has never realised that he's cured when he takes off his specs! He trips over everything, and never manages to walk through a door when he could walk into it.

You can be sure that 'Erbert will mistake everything he sees for something else, but his other senses are awesome. He can even recognise his friends by their taste.

THE BASH STREET PUPS

If you find yourself wandering along the alleyway beside the Bash Street junkyard, keep well clear of the large rubbish bin. It's home to a pack of nine stray mutts who are always getting into mischief. Their worst enemy is Clawdia, Walter's mean-spirited moggy.

BONES

Like Danny, Bones is the leader of the pack, but he doesn't always have a plan.

BLOTTY

Blotty finds it hard to make up his mind about anything.

'ENRY

'Enry's eyesight is so weak that he can't see past the end of his nose.

MANFRID

Shy little Manfrid uses his collar as a sort of comfort blanket, hiding his face behind it whenever he feels scared.

PEEPS

This wise young pup has great ideas and always knows what to do. The trouble is, the others don't always listen to her!

PUG

This pup is adorable despite his ugly mug – or perhaps because of it.

SNIFFY

Daft as a brush and short on brains, Sniffy has no common sense… or uncommon sense… or any sense at all.

TUBBY

With a snacktacular bone collection buried all over the alleyway, this food-loving pup is never far from a meal.

WIGGY

Wiggy's super-strong hair is spiky enough to spear up rubbish, and has scared off many another pup. Only one thing scares Wiggy – spiders!

WALTER WINTERBOTTOM (TEACHER)

FACT FILE

AGE: UNKNOWN

ADDRESS: A CLOSELY GUARDED SECRET

JOB: TEACHER, BASH STREET SCHOOL, CLASS 2B

STAR PUPIL: CUTHBERT

MOST DREADED PUPIL: DANNY

PRIZED POSSESSION: TEACHER-STRENGTH PAINKILLERS FOR CLASS 2B-STRENGTH HEADACHES

TOP SKILL: KEEPING HIS OLD BANGER OF A CAR RUNNING

FAMILY: MRS TEACHER

Teacher's main problem is that he really cares about educating his wild class. He has devoted his life to passing knowledge on to the next generation. It's a nice idea – if only they would listen!

EDNA CREECHER

Strict, grumpy and experienced at foiling pranks, Mrs Creecher is the only teacher who can handle Class 3C, which includes the likes of Dennis, Pieface, Roger the Dodger, JJ and Minnie. She's almost definitely human. Her thick glasses are the only reason the kids get away with their mischief. They never fail to take advantage of her blurry eyesight and they play all sorts of tricks on her. In fact, you could almost feel sorry for her – if she weren't so strict!

FACT FILE

AGE: NEVER YOU MIND

ADDRESS: DON'T BE NOSY

JOB: TEACHER, BASH STREET SCHOOL, CLASS 3C

STAR PUPIL: WALTER BROWN

MOST DREADED PUPIL: DENNIS MENACE

PRIZED POSSESSIONS: SCHOOL RULE BOOK, YELLOW KILT, SPORRAN

TOP SKILL: KNOWING ALL 923 SCHOOL RULES OFF BY HEART

FAMILY: NONE OF YOUR BUSINESS

MEGA STINK BOMB

OLIVE THE DINNERLADIES

What causes gas, groans and gurgling tummies? Yes, it's the Bash Street School dinner menu. Eat there at your own risk, and don't say we didn't warn you.

There are two dinnerladies at Bash Street School, and they're both called Olive. Everyone used to think that the first Olive was quite simply the worst cook in the world. The only person who enjoyed her food was Fatty, and even he struggled from time to time.

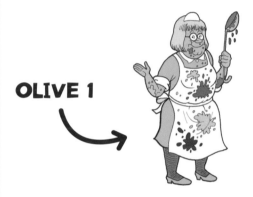

OLIVE 1

Then the school took in more pupils, and an extra pair of hands was required. To everyone's amazement and horror, Olive number two is just as bad a cook as Olive number one.

OLIVE 2

FACT FILE

OLIVE SPRAT/ORIGINAL OLIVE
ADDRESS: 24 CHUNK TERRACE
FAVOURITE PUPIL: FATTY
LEAST FAVOURITE PUPIL: WALTER BROWN, WHO GETS HIS MEALS SENT IN TO SCHOOL BY A PRIVATE CHEF
PRIZED POSSESSION: CONCRETE LADLE, THE ONLY THING STRONG ENOUGH TO SERVE HER SOUP
TOP SKILL: TURNING SCOFFABLE INGREDIENTS INTO STINKY SLOP
FAMILY: HUSBAND JACK, THE THINNEST MAN IN BEANOTOWN

FACT FILE

OLIVE PRATT/NEW OLIVE
ADDRESS: 57 HEINZ BOULEVARD
FAVOURITE PUPIL: PIEFACE
LEAST FAVOURITE PUPIL: CUTHBERT, WHO WILL ONLY EAT DRY TOAST
PRIZED POSSESSION: REINFORCED WOODEN SPOON, FOR STIRRING HER STODGY SAUCES
TOP SKILL: OVERCOOKING SALAD
FAMILY: SON BEN, AND DAUGHTER JERRY

ALF RAMSEY (MR JANITOR)

Mr Janitor works hard to look busy while actually doing as little as possible. He likes the school to be tidy, but he's a bit slapdash when it comes to details (and mopping). He's not as uptight as the teachers and often sees things from the kids' point of view.

He doesn't say much, but he notices everything, and no one knows the nooks, crannies and secret passages of the school as well as Mr Janitor does. Inside his office are years' worth of confiscated prankster gear, and he puts it to good use as he makes temporary repairs to all damage.

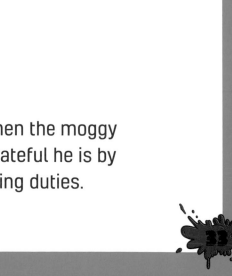

FACT FILE

ADDRESS: 69 SUTHERLAND ROAD
FAVOURITE PUPIL: ALL OF THEM
LEAST FAVOURITE PUPIL:
HE'S TOO EASY-GOING TO DISLIKE ANYONE
PRIZED POSSESSION: THE JANGLING KEYS HE WEARS ON HIS BELT
TOP SKILLS: SLOPPY MOPPING, BODGED REPAIRS, BREAKING UP FIGHTS
FAVOURITE FOOD:
OLIVE'S COTTAGE PIE – FOR FILLING IN THE CRACKS IN THE SCHOOL WALLS

WINSTON THE SCHOOL CAT

Mr Janitor found Winston in one of the school's wheelie bins. Since then the moggy has almost never left Mr Janitor's side. Winston likes to show how grateful he is by helping Mr Janitor with his work – especially when it comes to mopping duties.

33

BASH STREET SCHOOL

Most of the kids at Bash Street School are cunning, cool and totally up to date with the latest technology. However, some parts of the school haven't quite caught up with the 21st century yet. Actually, they're still finding the 20th century a bit too new-fangled...

It's a place of weird whiffs and nasty noises. A few of the teachers still wear mortar boards and gowns, and there are inkwells at every wooden table. In the staff room, the teachers relax by eating biscuits, drinking tea and coffee, and reading books about very, very hard sums.

One of Beanotown's best-kept secrets is the maze of tunnels beneath Bash Street School. If you can get past the kids, through the chewing-gum-lined corridors and down to the basement without being spotted, you'll find a mysterious old door in the janitor's office that leads to the tunnels.

As you tiptoe through the creepy tunnels, remember that you're treading in the footsteps of generations of brave kids who have escaped from boring lessons and strict teachers. The walls are lined with ancient carvings, and some say they look like ancient Menace graffiti.

No one wants to stay in the school for a second longer than necessary – not even the teachers. If you can make it past the strange clockwork robot, which looks suspiciously like Walter Brown, the tunnels will lead you to a place of safety and relaxation – the beach at Beanotown-on-Sea!

DID YOU KNOW?
The school has been rebuilt 24 times (so far) due to incidents including angry ducks, custard explosions, a runaway digger and Ant and Dec.

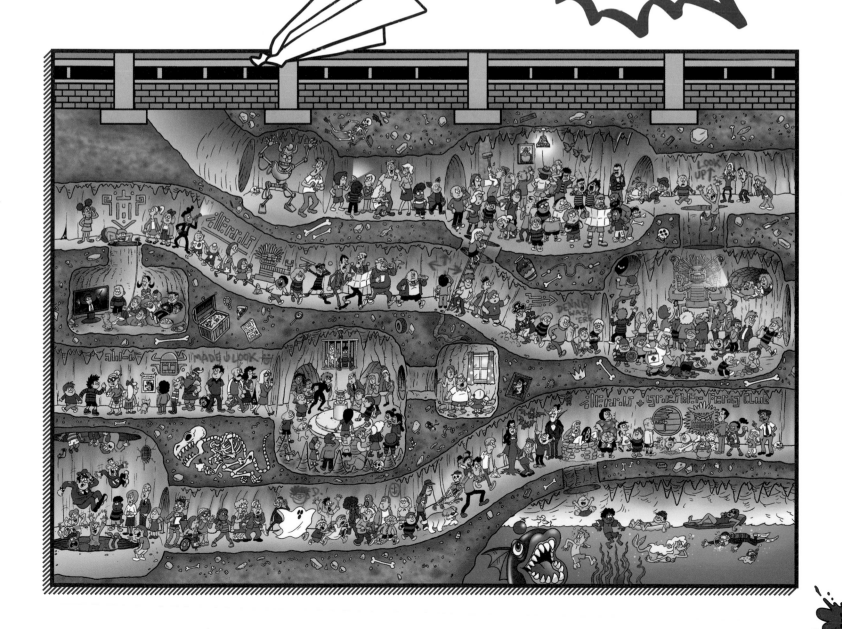

HORRIBLE HALL

Take our advice and steer well clear of the ruins of Horrible Hall during your visit. Long, long, LONG ago, when your dad was a boy, Horrible Hall was the school in Beanotown. Ever since it was mysteriously destroyed, a headless headmaster has haunted its ruins, searching for homework to mark and schoolchildren to punish.

Even the tourist guide is a g-g-ghost. And once you're in there, lost among the long corridors, it's really hard to find the way out. There are ghost teachers everywhere you turn.

Sometimes even the hall itself vanishes into thin air. And some of the Beanotown residents wish it would stay that way!

WHY IS THE HEADLESS HEADMASTER HEADLESS?

According to legend, he sent his own head to detention.

HOW TO RULE BASH STREET SCHOOL

If you're a kid and your parents are actually planning to send you to Bash Street School, **CONGRATULATIONS!** You're going to have the time of your life. Here are a few tips from the experts on thriving in this awesome school.

DON'T STOP YELLING UNTIL ALL THE OTHER KIDS HAVE OBEYED YOU.

ALWAYS TAKE YOUR MOST CHAOS-CAUSING PET TO SCHOOL.

TIP YOUR SCHOOLBOOKS OUT OF YOUR BAG AND FILL IT WITH SNACKS.

FIND A BEST FRIEND, JOIN A CLUB AND PRANK AT LEAST ONE PERSON A WEEK.

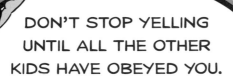

BE MORE PIRATE.

CARRY A PRANK KIT WITH YOU AT ALL TIMES. BASIC CONTENTS SHOULD INCLUDE A PEASHOOTER, A CATAPULT, ITCHING POWDER, A WHOOPEE CUSHION AND A STINK BOMB.

DO EVERYTHING I SAY AND YOU'LL BE FINE.

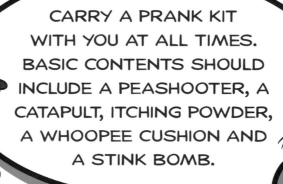

THE BROWN FAMILY

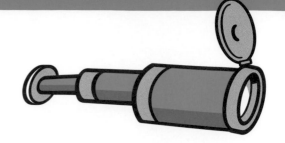

The Browns are some of the snootiest people in Beanotown. They think that they are above everyone else, and that the rules don't apply to them. The family consists of Walter, his parents Wilbur and Muriel, and his cat Clawdia.

WALTER MARGARET BROWN

Walter likes to hang out with people who are weaker and sillier than him – It makes him feel clever and important. He believes that he is perfect, and that he should decide what is right and what is wrong.

Tall and strong, Walter holds his head up high and enjoys bullying people who are small and weak. He's a tell-tale and a tease. Although he does well at school, he isn't a popular kid. Only Bertie realises how epic Walter really is, and gladly obeys him.

Walter has a mean streak. He encourages others to be naughty, but he makes sure no one can ever blame him. The one person Walter can never seem to get the better of is also his worst enemy. When he loses to Dennis and his temper flares up, people see the real Walter – a spoiled bully.

Walter looks down on childish things and thinks of himself as a mini adult. He dreams of being the Prime Minister one day. More than anything, Walter wants to impress his dad. Unfortunately, Mr Brown isn't impressed by losers – and Dennis beats Walter almost every time!

FACT FILE

BIRTHDAY:
9TH OCTOBER

ADDRESS: "TRANQUILITY",
53 GASWORKS ROAD

SCHOOL: BASH STREET SCHOOL,
CLASS 3C

LIKES: SPORTS, ANIMALS (BUT
ONLY THE PEDIGREE KIND)

DISLIKES:
BEING DISRESPECTED, DIRT,
MESS, BEING EMBARRASSED,
NOT BEING THE BEST, HAVING
TO LIVE NEXT DOOR TO DENNIS

BIGGEST FEAR: GNASHER

BEST QUALITY:
SELF-CONFIDENCE,
DETERMINATION TO BE
THE BEST

TOP SKILLS: FOCUSING ON
GETTING WHAT HE WANTS,
MANIPULATING OTHER PEOPLE,
BEING SLY

FAVOURITE FOOD:
ANYTHING EXPENSIVE FROM
A POSH RESTAURANT

UNSCRAMBLE THESE
LETTERS TO DISCOVER
ONE OF WALTER'S
FAVOURITE WORDS.

WROPE

POWER

DID YOU KNOW?
Walter has a private tutor
to make sure that he stays at the
top of the class, but he doesn't
want anyone to know
about that.

"I'M SUPERIOR IN EVERY WAY."

WHERE TO FIND WALTER
WHEN HE'S NOT SWOTTING FOR
HIS NEXT TEST, YOU MIGHT FIND
WALTER RELAXING IN HIS POOL AT
HOME, OR IN HIS ROOM PLOTTING
HIS REVENGE ON DENNIS.

WILBUR BROWN

The Mayor is the most important person in Beanotown – or at least that's what he thinks. He's big and strong, thanks to a daily workout in his home gym, and his hobbies include puffing out his chest and making other people feel small. Wilbur cares way too much about money, winning and what other people think.

Long ago, Wilbur asked Dennis's mum to marry him, but she refused and married Dennis's dad instead. That failure has haunted him all his life and he can't understand why Sandra Menace chose Dennis Sr over him… in fact, he can't understand people at all. Luckily, Sandra now works as his assistant and she has enough people skills for both of them.

It's Wilbur's dream to turn Beanotown into the kind of town that rich, important people would want to call home. The trouble is, that means sending annoying, noisy things like playgrounds, Bash Street School and Dennis out of town. We don't fancy his chances!

DID YOU KNOW?
Wilbur's first job was running his father's shop, Brown's TV Rentals and Aerials.

FACT FILE

BIRTHDAY: 16TH JANUARY
ADDRESS: "TRANQUILITY", 53 GASWORKS ROAD
JOB: MAYOR OF BEANOTOWN
LIKES: SUCKING UP TO PEOPLE WHO ARE MORE POWERFUL THAN HIM
DISLIKES: ANYONE WHO GETS IN HIS WAY
BIGGEST FEAR: FAILURE
BEST QUALITY: HARD WORKER
TOP SKILLS: MAKING MONEY
FAVOURITE FOOD: LOBSTER

MURIEL BROWN

"WILBUR FIRST."

Walter's mum believes in fitting in, supporting her family and keeping quiet. It's the simple things in life that make her happy, like watching soap operas and popping to the shops in her slippers. But Walter and his dad are embarrassed by things like that, so she keeps them secret.

Muriel had a good education, but Wilbur didn't want his wife to have a career. She fills her spare time by going to gym classes and worrying about her appearance. Because she lacks self-confidence, her own beliefs and ideas always come last.

FACT FILE
BIRTHDAY: 13TH SEPTEMBER
ADDRESS: "TRANQUILITY",
53 GASWORKS ROAD
JOB: HOUSEWIFE
LIKES: LOOKING AFTER HER
HUSBAND AND SON, SECRETLY
WATCHING TRASHY TV
DISLIKES: STANDING OUT,
SCRUFFY CLOTHES
BIGGEST FEAR: LETTING HER
FAMILY DOWN
BEST QUALITY: LOYALTY
TOP SKILLS: KNOWING THE
RULES IN ANY SITUATION
FAVOURITE FOOD: ITALIAN

CLAWDIA

This pure white snootcat is the family pet, and she looks elegant, respectable and well-trained. However, like her masters, her good manners are a mask. Underneath her beautiful surface she's every bit as vicious and scheming as Wilbur and Walter, and her temper is as sharp as her claws.

"HISSSSSS!"

DID YOU KNOW?
When she was a child, Muriel dreamed of being on the stage, but she never had quite enough confidence to make her dream come true.

PETER "PIEFACE" SHEPHERD

One of Dennis's best friends, Pieface got his name because of his favourite food in the whole world. Pieface is kind and funny, and he loves making people happy.

Pieface has a very special pet – Paul the potato. Yes, you read that right. Paul may be just a humble potato, but Pieface talks to him, takes him to the park and loves him very much.

"THERE'S NOTHING YOU CAN'T PUT IN A PIE!"

FACT FILE

AGE: 10
ADDRESS: 62 GASWORKS AVENUE
SCHOOL: BASH STREET SCHOOL, CLASS 3C
LIKES: EATING PIES, MUSIC, WATCHING CHERRY BAKEWELL'S BAKING SHOW ON TV
DISLIKES: UNKINDNESS, MATHS
BIGGEST FEAR: SOGGY PIES
BEST QUALITY: BEING A GREAT FRIEND
TOP SKILLS: KNOWING WHAT'S IN A PIE JUST BY FEELING THE CRUST, INVENTING NEW PIES
FAVOURITE FOOD: PIES, OF COURSE!

"YES, WALTER."

FACT FILE

AGE: 10
ADDRESS: 28 BAXENDALE CLOSE
SCHOOL: BASH STREET SCHOOL, CLASS 3C
LIKES: HIS PET SNAKES, PICTURES OF HORSES
DISLIKES: RIDING HORSES
BIGGEST FEAR: LOOKING STUPID
BEST QUALITY: HE'S NOT AS MEAN AS WALTER
TOP SKILLS: TALE-TELLING, OBEYING WALTER, INSULTING OTHERS
FAVOURITE FOOD: PIZZA

BERTIE BLENKINSOP

Bertie Blenkinsop would probably call himself Walter's best friend. Walter would be more likely to use the word "henchman" since Bertie always does whatever Walter orders.

The rich Blenkinsops have owned Beanotown Gas for years, and Bertie knows that he will never have to work hard to earn a living. Like Walter, he looks down on people who don't have as much as he does. However, he isn't as cruel as Walter, and the other kids in Class 3C can sometimes get through to him when Walter's not around.

JJ

"GIVE IT YOUR ALL!"

You might find JJ at the skatepark, doing some crazy drumming with the Dinmakers, or just zooming through Beanotown on her BMX. Wherever she is, you can bet that she's doing something fast and energetic. JJ loves sports – she's fit and fearless enough to try anything, and right now she can't decide whether she wants to be a PE teacher or an explorer.

JJ's best friends are Rubi, Dennis and Pieface, and she loves hanging out with all of them. Dennis makes her laugh more than anyone because he'll do anything for a bit of fun. JJ takes sports very seriously, but she also knows the value of a good prank – she runs a secret shop at school where she sells pranks to the other kids.

FACT FILE

AGE: 16TH SEPTEMBER
ADDRESS: GASWORKS ROAD
SCHOOL: BASH STREET SCHOOL, CLASS 3C
LIKES: WINNING, DRUMMING, SPORTS, HELPING PEOPLE
DISLIKES: LOSING, LAZINESS, BULLIES
BIGGEST FEAR: FAILING
BEST QUALITY: SHE NEVER GIVES UP
TOP SKILLS: SPORTS, STANDING UP FOR HERSELF AND HER FRIENDS
FAVOURITE FOOD: FRUIT

DID YOU KNOW?
When she was younger, JJ's four older brothers were too big and fast for her to be able to play with them. Nowadays, they're still bigger than her, but she's the fastest of them all!

BILLY WHIZZ

If you see a red blur speeding along faster than you can blink, it's likely to be Billy Whizz. When he first started running as a toddler, he went so fast that his nappy began to smoke! He's a kind boy, although he does have a temper, and he can be a bit impatient. His greatest heroes are Mo Farah and Usain Bolt.

Billy lives with his parents and his little brother Alfie, who really makes him laugh. His pet tortoise, Millie, might seem like an odd pet for the fastest boy on Earth, but there are no dogs who could keep up with him.

Billy gets on well with the other Beanotown kids, when he can slow down for long enough to play with them. Although he's not as much of a prankster as Minnie, Dennis and Roger, he has been known to use his amazing speed to get his own back from time to time!

DID YOU KNOW?
The soles of Billy's trainers are made from Formula One car tyres.

FACT FILE

AGE: 10
ADDRESS: GASWORKS ROAD
SCHOOL: BASH STREET SCHOOL, CLASS 3C
LIKES: PE CLASS, ATHLETICS, RELAY RACES
DISLIKES: WAITING, STROLLING, WALKING
BIGGEST FEAR: HIS TRAINERS WEARING OUT
BEST QUALITY: ALWAYS FINISHING FIRST
TOP SKILLS: MOVING SO QUICKLY THAT HE CAN TRAVEL BACK IN TIME
FAVOURITE FOOD: FAST FOOD

BETTY AND THE YETI

"OH NO, YETI!"

Betty has a secret. A BIG secret. Her best friend is huge, hairy… and definitely not human. Betty and Yeti first met at a campsite, when they made friends over a comic. Betty managed to sneak Yeti onto the roof rack of her dad's car, among all the suitcases, and ever since then he has been a proud Beanotown resident.

Betty loves sharing her life with Yeti. She includes him in everything she does and cares for him when he's poorly. Yeti has learned to speak English – sort of. He tries all the things Betty loves, from yoga and singing to drawing and playing in the park. Sometimes he is a bit confused by life, but to be fair to Yeti, life in Beanotown is very confusing.

FACT FILE

BETTY
AGE: 7
ADDRESS: 8 BAGGE-SHOTT WYNDE
SCHOOL: HOME SCHOOLED
LIKES: DRESSING UP, BALLET, GLITTER, HEARTS, SPARKLES, YETI
DISLIKES: NOT GETTING HER OWN WAY
BIGGEST FEAR: HER DAD FINDING OUT ABOUT YETI
BEST QUALITY: CARING
TOP SKILLS: GIVING ORDERS, TAKING CONTROL
FAVOURITE FOOD: ICE CREAM IN A CONE

FACT FILE

YETI
AGE: NOBODY KNOWS – COULD BE ANYTHING FROM 7 TO 700
ADDRESS: A LARGE HIDING PLACE IN BETTY'S HOUSE
SCHOOL: DON'T BE SILLY – HE'S A YETI!
LIKES: BETTY, DISGUISES
DISLIKES: BEING TOO HOT
BIGGEST FEAR: YETI HUNTERS
BEST QUALITY: GOOD LEARNER
TOP SKILLS: STRENGTH, DISGUISING HIMSELF
FAVOURITE FOOD: CAKE

RUBIDIUM VON SCREWTOP (RUBI)

Rubi is amazingly clever. When she's not hanging out with Dennis, JJ and Pieface, she loves experimenting with science, inventing cool new gadgets and practising stunts in her one-of-a-kind wheelchair. She also plays in the Dinmakers.

She is super-inspired by her dad, Professor von Screwtop, who is the head scientist at Beanotown's top secret research lab. Rubi has watched him doing experiments so many times that now she does them even better! She knows that she can always raid his store room, which is full of bits and bobs that she can use for her projects.

Rubi uses her tablet to find out information about anything and everything, and she loves learning new things. Her inventions and ideas often get her friends out of trouble, and she's never afraid to give them her opinion while she's helping them!

"I HAVE THE ANSWER!"

DID YOU KNOW?
Rubi has customised her chair with the latest tech. Her awesome hacks include an all-terrain drive motor, solar panels, a satnav, built-in wifi and a fridge for super-cold fizzy drinks.

FACT FILE
AGE: 10
ADDRESS: 112 MERCER STREET
SCHOOL: BASH STREET SCHOOL, CLASS 3C
LIKES: SCIENCE, WHEELCHAIR STUNTS, FACTS
DISLIKES: BEING CALLED BY HER FULL NAME
BIGGEST FEAR: PEOPLE THINKING THAT BEING IN A WHEELCHAIR MIGHT SLOW HER DOWN
BEST QUALITY: INDEPENDENCE
TOP SKILLS: WHEELCHAIR STUNT PERFORMANCE, TECH INVENTIONS, KEYBOARD PLAYING
FAVOURITE FOOD: SUSHI

LORD SNOOTY

Lord Snooty is a somewhat misleading nickname for Earl Marmaduke of Bunkerton. He didn't choose to be a lord, he was simply born into it. The ten-year-old toff lives in Bunkerton Castle – also called The Pink Palace. Snooty has never met his parents and nobody truly knows their story. Every year on his birthday and at Christmas he receives cards with two handwritten xs on them – plus a cheque for ten million pounds. He's well looked after by his legal guardian, his butler, Parkinson. Parkinson is also a keen comic artist who dreams of one day being accomplished enough to draw for the Beano comic.

To Walter Brown's disgust, E-MOB (Snooty's security codename) is by far the richest individual in Beanotown. It annoys Walter that Marmaduke seems more interested in making pals with the kids from Bash Street School than with the mayor's genuinely 'snooty' son. Walter's dream is to attend a sleepover at the castle. He imagines a luxury four-poster bed and butler service because he's simply made for that life. The funny thing is, Snooty would rather hang out with one of his secret buddies from Class 2B, using the antique beds as trampolines.

Snooty will often secretly pay for some of the kids' wilder mischief to be repaired. It's a little-known secret that he personally paid for Bash Street School to be rebuilt, after it had been demolished by Ant and Dec (yes, *that* Ant and Dec!).

FACT FILE

BIRTHDAY: 30TH JULY
ADDRESS: BUNKERTON CASTLE
LIKES: HANGING OUT WITH THE KIDS FROM BASH STREET SCHOOL
DISLIKES: SNOBS AND POSH PEOPLE
BIGGEST FEAR: LONELINESS
BEST QUALITY: GENEROSITY
TOP SKILLS: FIXING SCRATCHES ON ANTIQUE FURNITURE WITH A BROWN FELT TIP PEN
FAVOURITE FOOD: BEANS, CAVIAR AND CHIPS WASHED DOWN WITH A VINTAGE COLA

THE DAWSON FAMILY

The Dawsons live on Gasworks Road with their family pet, Dodgecat. Ada and Les have always followed the rules, and they dislike trying anything new. That's probably why their son, Roger, is so very inventive!

ROGER THE DODGER

This sneaky kid always has a trick up his sleeve. he has a library of 850 old Dodge Books in his attic, and even more information in his own private DodgeWiki, on his DodgePad. He uses his wits and does things his own way – or gets out of doing them altogether!

Roger can't stand doing things the easy way. He takes pride in surprising everyone and doing the unexpected. It's a way of life for him, and it means that he hardly ever lets anyone in on his plans – except for his best friends Dennis and Minnie, of course. Roger, Dennis and Minnie all do things very differently, though. Roger loves planning his pranks and Dennis and Minnie often depend on him being super organised – the opposite of them!

"I CAN DODGE THIS!"

UNSCRAMBLE THESE LETTERS TO DISCOVER ONE OF ROGER'S FAVOURITE WORDS.

VIKINGS

SKIVING

FACT FILE

BIRTHDAY: 18TH APRIL

ADDRESS: 14 GASWORKS ROAD

SCHOOL: BASH STREET SCHOOL, CLASS 3C

LIKES: SKIVING, TRICKS, DODGEWIKI

DISLIKES: HARD WORK, DOING WHAT HE'S BEEN ASKED TO DO, EARLY MORNINGS

BIGGEST FEAR: HAVING TO DO ANYTHING THE WAY MOST PEOPLE DO IT

BEST QUALITY: NEVER GIVING UP

TOP SKILLS: PLANNING DODGES, AVOIDING HARD WORK

FAVOURITE FOOD: JAMMY BISCUITS

WHERE TO FIND ROGER

ROGER IS SO UNPREDICTABLE THAT YOU CAN NEVER GUESS WHERE HIS DODGES WILL TAKE HIM, BUT SOONER OR LATER HE'LL TURN UP AT HOME FOR HIS NOSH, SO HEAD TO 14 GASWORKS ROAD AT TEA TIME!

DID YOU KNOW?

Roger doesn't just think up dodges for himself, so if there's anything you need to avoid, head over to his dodge den and he'll come up with the perfect dodge for you.

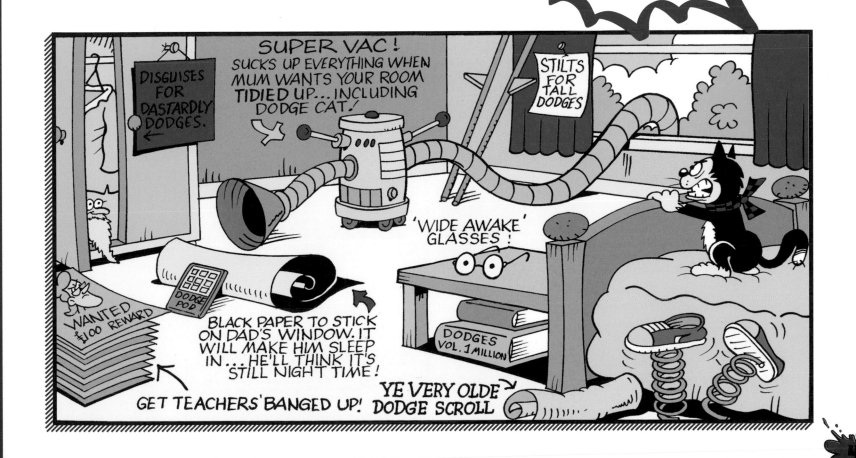

ADA DAWSON

"HURRY UP!"

Roger's mum is always in a hurry. She is quick and efficient and she likes things to be done briskly and well, all while following the rules.

Ada loves zooming along in her sports car and hearing the sound of its tyres screeching on the road. She finds Roger hard to understand. He never wants to follow the rules and his laid-back attitude is very different from her bustling style.

FACT FILE
BIRTHDAY: 31ST OCTOBER
ADDRESS: 14 GASWORKS ROAD
JOB: COUNCIL TAX COLLECTION, SCRIMP TOWERS
LIKES: COFFEE, FAST CARS
DISLIKES: BEING DISORGANISED
BIGGEST FEAR: LOSING THINGS
BEST QUALITY: BEING METHODICAL
TOP SKILLS: PEOPLE MANAGEMENT
FAVOURITE FOOD: SAUSAGES AND BAKED BEANS

LES DAWSON

Roger's dad is a nice man who always tries to do the right thing. The trouble is, he thinks he knows the best way to do everything, and he won't try anything different.

He loves his job, where he gets to make sure that every paperclip is made in exactly the right way. He wishes that his son could see how much better life is when you follow the rules.

"YOU CAN'T DODGE EVERYTHING, SON."

FACT FILE
BIRTHDAY: 25TH JUNE
ADDRESS: 14 GASWORKS ROAD
JOB: ASSEMBLY LINE MANAGER AT PERKINS' PAPERCLIP FACTORY
LIKES: CONTROLLING EVERYTHING TO MAKE THINGS NICE FOR EVERYONE
DISLIKES: CHAOS, NOT BEING IN CONTROL
BIGGEST FEAR: THE UNKNOWN
BEST QUALITY: PATIENCE
TOP SKILLS: PLANNING, MANAGING, CONTROLLING, MODEL-MAKING
FAVOURITE FOOD: BAKED BEANS AND SAUSAGES

DODGE CAT

Roger's pet knows a few dodges of his own – mostly to get himself out of trips to the vet. He sometimes gets into mischief with Chester and Winston, but like Roger he prefers a laid-back life.

THE DINMAKERS

The fastest and loudest garage rock band in Beanotown practises in Dennis's den in Beanotown Woods. They're loud, raw, passionate and energetic. (Did we mention they're loud?)

DENNIS
PLAYS THE LEAD GUITAR AND SINGS.

GNASHER
RATTLES THE MARACAS AND DANCES.

PIEFACE
PLAYS THE BASS GUITAR.

JJ
PLAYS THE DRUMS.

RUBI
PLAYS THE SYNTHESISER, SEQUENCER AND SAMPLER.

ROGER
SOMETIMES JOINS THE DINMAKERS AS A SPECIAL GUEST PERFORMER.

DANGEROUS DAN

Dan probably knew that you were coming to Beanotown before you did. He might look like an innocent schoolboy, but in fact he's a highly trained secret agent. He always wears a tuxedo, which contains all the latest gadgets and gizmos to help him defeat his enemies.

Talking of enemies, Dan is always on the lookout for agents of SMIRK – the Secret Ministry of Intelligent Rotters Komittee. They would love to defeat Dan and break into Spy HQ, but he always manages to get the better of them.

Dan is watched over by Agent Q, who gives him his missions and trains him. But most of the time, Dan uses his extraordinary skills to do the most ordinary things, like sneaking in late to school!

"I'VE GOT A PLOT TO FOIL!"

TOP SECRET

FACT FILE

AGE: 10

ADDRESS: 12 GREENBELT DRIVE

SCHOOL: BASH STREET SCHOOL, CLASS 3C

LIKES: TRYING OUT NEW GADGETS, GETTING A MISSION, FOOTBALL, SECRET CODES

DISLIKES: CHANGING HIS SOCKS, SUDOKU

BIGGEST FEAR: PEOPLE FINDING OUT HIS SECRETS (SO SHHH!)

BEST QUALITY: HE ALWAYS BELIEVES IN HIMSELF

TOP SKILL: FIGHTING EVIL SCHEMES, FOILING SMIRK AGENTS

FAVOURITE FOOD: MINCE SPIES

DID YOU KNOW?
Dan's dad, JB, is also a secret agent. Not even Dan's mum, Darlene, knows his real name!

TRICKY DICKY

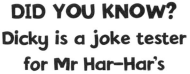

Dicky lives with his parents and his big sister, Fran. He lives for practical jokes – not a day goes past without someone getting pranked by this cheeky chortler. Dicky is a cheerful, good-natured boy, and his harmless pranks often stop bullies and teach rude people a lesson. His teacher has no sense of humour, but that just makes Dicky try even harder!

FACT FILE

AGE: 8

ADDRESS: 34 NUTTYTOWN ROAD

SCHOOL: BASH STREET SCHOOL, MR THROBB'S CLASS

LIKES: PRANKING PEOPLE WITH HIS BEST FRIENDS, MIKEY AND DAZ

DISLIKES: BULLIES, PEOPLE TAKING LIFE TOO SERIOUSLY

BIGGEST FEAR: LOSING HIS COLLECTION OF PRACTICAL JOKES

BEST QUALITY: SEEING THE FUNNY SIDE OF THINGS

TOP SKILLS: HE CAN WIN ANY PRANKING CONTEST

FAVOURITE FOOD: EXPLODING SAUSAGES

DID YOU KNOW?
Dicky is a joke tester for Mr Har–Har's Joke Shop.

"PRANKS FOR THE MEMORIES!"

JOKE BOX

ERIC WIMP (BANANAMAN)

"BE PREPARED."

At first glance, Eric doesn't seem very special. He's puny, shy and not at all interested in pranking people. He just wants to live a peaceful life. But Eric has an incredible secret. When he eats a banana, he becomes Bananaman, an adult superhero with phenomenally huge strength – and a phenomenally small brain. When Bananaman looks in the mirror he sees the most handsome, clever, funny and humble superhero the world has ever known.

Eric tries to get on with life, but he never knows when Police Chief O'Reilly will call him on the bananaphone. Whenever Beanotown is in danger, Bananaman is there to (try to) put things right. His most trusted friend is Crow, who is secretly the brains behind the banana. However much Bananaman might bungle a mission, he manages to come out on top and lives to fly another day.

DID YOU KNOW?
Eric has a crush on Fiona the newsreader.

FACT FILE

AGE: 10
ADDRESS: 29 ACACIA ROAD
SCHOOL: BASH STREET SCHOOL
LIKES: RISK, PUNS, SAVING PEOPLE
DISLIKES: VILLAINS
BIGGEST FEAR: RUNNING OUT OF HEROIC FEATS TO ACHIEVE
BEST QUALITY: COURAGE
TOP SKILLS: USING THE TOOLS ON HIS BANANABELT, FLYING

WHERE TO FIND BANANAMAN
YOU'LL FIND BANANAMAN WHEREVER THERE'S A VILLAIN TRYING TO DESTROY BEANOTOWN. (AND AFTERWARDS YOU'LL FIND ERIC RECOVERING AT HOME.)

54

BANANAMAN'S FIENDISH FOES

CALAMITY JAMES

Take our advice and give Beanotown's unluckiest boy a wide berth. He has a knack for attracting unlikely accidents, tripping over things and missing out on amazing chances. There is a bed permanently reserved for him in the local hospital.

James lives with his best friend and pet Alexander Lemming, his mumsie, and his terrible bad luck. The Squelchy Things love him because funny and disastrous things are always happening to him, and you are most likely to spot one of them by hanging out with James. However, that's a risk that's probably not worth taking.

FACT FILE

AGE: 9

ADDRESS: 13 LUCKY LANE

SCHOOL: BASH STREET SCHOOL, NEAR THE BOTTOM OF CLASS IA

LIKES: LUCKY CHARMS (THEY NEVER WORK)

DISLIKES: HIS BAD LUCK

BIGGEST FEAR: NOTHING. WHAT'S THE WORST THAT COULD HAPPEN?

BEST QUALITY: ENDLESS OPTIMISM, RESILIENCE

TOP SKILLS: NEVER GIVING UP, EVEN WHEN HE REALLY, REALLY SHOULD

FAVOURITE FOOD: CORNFLAKES

"MY LUCK IS CHANGING!"

DID YOU KNOW?
James has a crush on Minnie the Minx.

LURKING UNSEEN

Some of Beanotown's residents are rarely, or never, seen. If you glimpse a Squelchy Thing or a Numskull, consider yourself lucky!

DID YOU KNOW?
There are also Tumskulls (stomach department) and Bumskulls. Let's stop right there.

NUMSKULLS

Everyone in Beanotown has tiny versions of themselves living inside their bodies. They help to make sure that bodies work the way they should.

BRAINY (BRAIN DEPARTMENT)

BLINKY (EYE DEPARTMENT)

SNITCH (NOSE DEPARTMENT)

CRUNCHER (MOUTH DEPARTMENT)

RADAR (EAR DEPARTMENT)

SQUELCHY THINGS

These wobbly, squishy little creatures were accidentally created by Professor Crackpott, and set free by Calamity James.

SQUELCH!

GUZZLE! GORGE! STUFF!

CRAM!

BOING!

BOING! SQUELCH!

SQUELCHY FACTS

THEY ARE THE FASTEST BREEDING AND MUTATING LIFE-FORM ON EARTH.

NO TWO SQUELCHIES ARE EXACTLY THE SAME.

SQUELCHY THINGS LIVE UNDERGROUND AND VISIT THE SURFACE TO LAUGH AT THE PEOPLE OF BEANOTOWN.

THEY LOVE PRANKS AND JOKES, SO KIDS ARE THEIR FAVOURITE HUMANS.

HUMANS CANNOT SEE SQUELCHY THINGS BUT ANIMALS CAN.

SQUELCHY THINGS CAN'T COUNT.

YOU SHOULD NEVER PUT SALT ON A SQUELCHY THING.

HOW TO BE A TOP BEANOTOWN RESIDENT

So you like Beanotown so much that you're thinking of moving here? Great! It's an awesome place to live... as long as you know how to manage its wacky ways. Even though it's a friendly place, you'll find that there is quite a lot of accidental damage. One thing every Beanotown resident learns is how to bodge DIY without spending a penny.

MAKE FRIENDS WITH DENNIS MENACE.

REMEMBER THAT ANYTHING COULD HAPPEN (AND IT PROBABLY WILL).

STAY ALERT FOR ACCIDENTS WHEN YOU'RE WITH CALAMITY JAMES.

NEVER ASK, "WHAT'S THE WORST THAT CAN HAPPEN?"

TIE BROKEN DRAINPIPES IN PLACE WITH AN OLD SOCK.

NEVER TRUST THE MAYOR!

TO REPAIR A BROKEN ROOF, PUSH AN UMBRELLA THROUGH THE HOLE AND THEN OPEN IT.

USE STICKY TAPE TO HOLD BROKEN WINDOW PANES TOGETHER.

FILL POTHOLES WITH ROAD-COLOURED JELLY.

BEANOTOWN FRIENDSHIP

THE GNASH BASH

Dennis and his friends share a special, fun greeting filled with slaps, bumps and exploding fists. It's much too complicated for grown-ups to learn. See if you can master it!

1. BUMP YOUR FISTS TOGETHER.

2. SLAP EACH OTHER'S RIGHT HAND AND HOLD ON TIGHT.

3. SLAP EACH OTHER'S LEFT HAND AND THEN LET GO OF EACH OTHER.

4. FIST BUMP, WITH EACH PERSON STICKING UP THEIR LITTLE FINGER.

5. FIST BUMP, WITH EACH PERSON STICKING UP THEIR FOREFINGER AND LITTLE FINGER LIKE A BULL'S HORNS.

6. EXPLODE YOUR FISTS APART.

DID YOU KNOW?
Walter and his friends have a secret handshake to try to make others feel left out. It's so boring and grown-up that no one else is interested in learning it!

BEANOTOWN'S HISTORY

BEANOTOWN'S VIKING PAST

Thanks to his secret clock tower time machine, Dennis once discovered something amazing about Beanotown's history.

Dennis was curious when he heard that Beanotown Museum was going to defrost a frozen Viking. When it turned out that the Viking was wearing a red-and-black jersey and had a dog, he had to know more!

Using the time machine, Dennis and Gnasher zoomed back in time to 801 AD. Vikings had just arrived in the area, which was ruled by a tribe of people who looked strangely like Walter and his dad. It turned out that Vikings are great guys to have on your side when times are tough. Dennis and Gnasher fitted right in!

The Vikings got on with the tribe at first, but things soon changed...

When battle broke out over a loo roll and a few magic beans, Dennis led a pack of Viking avengers to victory. This was the start of one of the longest-running feuds in history – Menaces versus Browns.

The Vikings turned Beanotown into the awesome place it is today. They even built the secret tunnels that connect the caves under the town. If you explore them, keep your eyes peeled for the ancient carvings and see if you recognise the boy and his tripe hound...

With the future of Beanotown assured, Dennis sledged into a glacier and became trapped in the ice. He was defrosted by Beanotown Museum 1000 years later.

Thaw-some!

DID YOU KNOW?
One of Minnie's ancestors was a member of the original Viking raiding party.

60

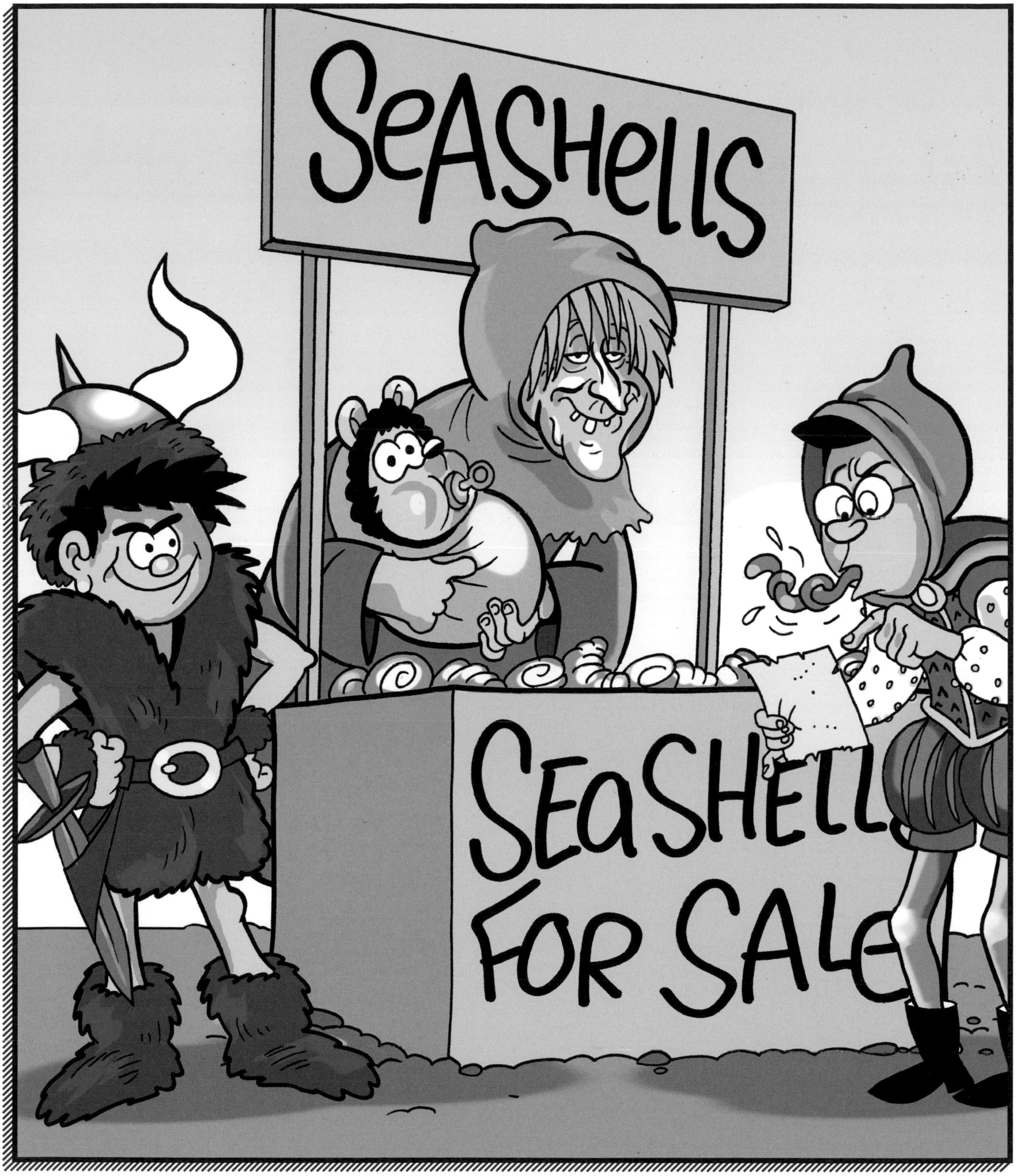
SEASHELLS
SEASHELLS FOR SALE

WHERE TO GO

MOUNT BEANO

DID YOU KNOW?
Mount Beano stands at an impressive 1938 metres tall!

Towering above Beanotown, Mount Beano is a part of the life of every single Beanotown resident.
For some, it's a place of fun, excitement and adventure. For others, it's just the first thing they see as they escape through the windows of Bash Street School.

To reach Mount Beano, head through the woods, past Dennis's den and beyond the grassy foothills. Many explorers have scaled its snowy slopes, searching for Yeti. They have no idea that he is living with Betty!

One of the highlights of the year is Beanotown's Freewheeler Derby. Dennis loves taking part in this gravity-powered, rule-free race down Mount Beano.

Mount Beano is at the heart of all sorts of exciting challenges, from nature survival tests and races to the summit, to hikes where you can discover mysterious places. Don't miss this snow-tacular spot!

DANGER!

LAKE MESS

From a distance, Lake Mess looks like a tranquil beauty spot. And from a distance is probably the best way to enjoy it. If you're looking for time out and a few hours of peaceful fishing, then this is not the place for you. Up close, this place is... well... a mess.

No one knows for certain what secrets lurk inside Lake Mess. But the gigantic footprints on the muddy banks tell their own story…

Even if you can ignore the warning signs, rusty bicycle wheels and unwanted wellies in the water, something is bound to shatter the silence. It could be the yells of Mr Dawson as he discovers Roger's latest dodge for getting out of baiting the hooks. Or it could be your own squeals as you run from the monster!

DID YOU KNOW?
Lake Mess can be found behind Beanotown Woods.

WHERE TO GO

BEANOTOWN-ON-SEA

DID YOU KNOW?
This is also the spot where the Beanotown Spring bubbles up.

Why travel abroad for your summer holidays when you have a wicked beach right on the doorstep? Beanotown-on-Sea is the perfect spot for a summer holiday with its annual Sand Sculpture Championship.

When you've struggled through the underground tunnels from Bash Street School, you'll eventually find yourself blinking in the sunlight near a huge, red-and-black lighthouse. You have arrived in Beanotown-on-Sea! The lighthouse is a great place to hide because none of the teachers has enough puff to get all the way to the top. It's also the first sign that tells tourists when Dennis is home. If the lights are on, he's around!

WHAT TO DO

BEANOTOWN BURGERS

DID YOU KNOW?
Fatty Brown is banned from the lunchtime buffet.

When you get hungry, head over to Beanotown Burgers.

It doesn't look like much on the outside. And it doesn't look like much on the inside, either. But the burgers taste awesome! Like most shops here, Beanotown Burgers has adjusted to being in such a special place. There's a mop that staff grab as soon as they spot Calamity James, and even a mini cannon so that they can shoot food at Billy Whizz.

CINEMA

There is always something to watch in Beanotown, but sometimes people want to escape from real life.

Beanotown's cinema is like a palace – it's huge, it's ancient and it hasn't changed for years. The floor is sticky, the service is grumpy and the prices give Dennis's dad panic attacks, but it's an experience you'll never forget.

65

SPORT AND LEISURE

LIBRARY

Beanotown has an epic new library in the place of the old supermarket. With a lift, a slide, a yoga zone and a massive collection of books, it's the perfect place to relax and gather information.

The biggest sections are books about mischief and DIY repairs. People in Beanotown don't just enjoy mayhem – they enjoy reading about it too. A few of the librarians find it hard to accept that they live in the 21st century now. People keep telling them that modern libraries have computers, noisy events and cake, but they still hiss "Shhh!" if you make a sound. Luckily the head librarian, Betty's Yeti's uncle, thinks that libraries should be fun, happy and noisy places.

LIBRARY GHOST

The old library is still open, but it is barely used. That's partly because of the deadly boring books on the shelves, but mostly because of the ghost librarian.

The ghost librarian has sworn to protect the humungous Book of Beanotown Secrets. It's a whopper because Beanotown has such a lot of secrets. The town's mischief makers would love to get their hands on that volume!

MUSEUM

If it's old, Beanotown Museum has got it. From frozen mammoths to statues and suits of armour, you'll find the whole history of Beanotown inside these crumbling walls.

This is a great place to learn about the town's past, and to avoid pranksters. Dennis and his friends usually prefer whizzing around on their skateboards and playing in the treehouse to gazing at models of cavemen, broken pieces of clay and a load of old dinosaur bones. As Minnie points out, living dinosaurs are way more interesting.

General Blight and Doctor Gloom occasionally hatch a plot to raid the museum and steal all its dusty old treasures. Luckily, Bananaman always arrives in the nick of time, cracks a couple of terrible puns and delivers the baddies to Beanotown Jail.

SKATE PARK

Beanotown skate park is one of the most popular hangouts in Beanotown, and you can usually find several pranksters showing off on the ramps. It's right in front of Bash Street School, which is unfair for two reasons:

DID YOU KNOW? Once, Mayor Wilbur Brown managed to close the skate park down.

1. THE KIDS CAN SEE IT FROM THEIR CLASSROOM WINDOWS.

2. IF THEY TRIED TO SNEAK OUT TO USE IT, THEIR TEACHERS WOULD SPOT THEM STRAIGHT AWAY.

Dennis's Favourite Tricks

Ollie – the oldest trick in the book, but it's a classic.

Kickflip – learning this helped Dennis to learn other flip tricks.

Frontside/Backside Powerslide – this was one of the first slides Dennis mastered.

360 Flip – it feels great when you land this trick.

Wallride – this looks so cool.

Darkslide – super hard to pull off but looks amazeballs.

POOL

The swimming pool's Banana Flume is the most awesome slide in Beanotown. Based on a dog's intestines, it's bigger, faster (and more likely to make you feel sick) than any other slide in town.

DUCK ISLAND

The small, innocent-looking island in the middle of Beanotown Park's duck pond is one of the most incredible places in Beanotown. It's bigger on the inside, and if you set so much as a toenail on it, you're likely to face a Jurassic-sized problem. Dennis and his friends, Dennis's dad and Walter have been there and made it out again. (Dennis's dad and Walter have blocked out the memories.)

The real reason for Duck Island's mysteries is an asteroid that hit it 65 million years ago. It created a compression field, squashing everything on the island to a fraction of its size. There is a machine around the asteroid that keeps it small. If it ever broke, Duck Island would spread out across the country.

No one can say for certain how big Duck Island really is. What they can say for certain (in trembling voices) is what they saw: there are dinosaurs, Vikings, a gigantic dog who looks uncannily like Gnasher, a volcano and evidence of an ancient civilisation.

DID YOU KNOW?
Dennis's gran knows all about Duck Island, as she discovered it when she was a young mischief-maker herself.

BEANOTOWN PARK

Beanotown Park sits between Dennis's house and Lord Snooty's castle.

It's a beautiful spot, with the duck pond in the middle and plenty of trees, flowers and bushes. It's also the scene of countless pranks, tricks, jokes, dodges and disasters. Don't spend too long sitting on a park bench, or you're likely to get tangled up in someone's hair-raising scheme.

DID YOU KNOW?
Parky Bowles is the park keeper, and from his hut among the flower beds he fights a losing a battle against daily tricks and pranks.

BEANOLAND

Beanotown's awesome amusement park is next to the beach, and it's crammed with puketrifying and petrifying rides, from the Beanotron 4000 rollercoaster to the bouncy Bunkerton Castle, the rally race cars and the ghostly Helter Skeletor. Best of all, thanks to the generosity of Lord Snooty, it's all free!

ZOO

Everyone loves a trip to the zoo, but in Beanotown it can sometimes be a bit of a risky day out.

For one thing, there is a large, red button on display that opens all the cages at the same time. (The zookeeper admits that this may have been a bad idea.) At least one person has pressed it just to find out what would happen. What happened was utter mayhem. (We won't name names, but the boy in question had a stripy top and a dog with hair like barbed wire.)

The animal with the most escapes under his trunk is Ellis the elephant. Dennis admires his determination to succeed and helps him whenever possible. His dad doesn't approve. He thinks that Dennis and Ellis are a bad influence on each other.

DID YOU KNOW?
Wilbur Brown owns a controlling share in Beanotown Zoo.

FOOTBALL STADIUM: COLD TRAFFORD

Also known as the Theatre of Screams, this is the home of Beanotown United. The players have super-loyal fans who cheer them on year after year as they battle to avoid relegation.

WILDLIFE

Beanotown's wildlife is a little wilder than most. Use this spotter's guide to tick off all the creatures you see during your visit.

WORM YOGHURT

SEWER CREATURES ☐

Grasping beasties slither their slimy tentacles through Beanotown's drain covers, searching for scraps of food and tripping up passers-by as an added bonus.

BIRDS ☐

Beanotown birds are as quirky as the people and the pets. You might see them sipping drinks as they fly along or even wearing clothes.

MYSTERY CREATURES ☐

Watch out for eerie eyes peering at you from inside small gaps and post box slots. You will never get an explanation.

LAKE MESS MONSTER ☐

This gargantuan beast lives in Lake Mess and is rarely seen.

RODNEY THE RAM ☐

Rodney provides the red wool for Dennis's beloved jumper. He lives high up on Mount Beano amid the snow and ice.

DAVE THE GOAT ☐

Dave is good friends with Rodney, and also lives at the top of Mount Beano.

MR FROSTY ☐

Mr Frosty, a 365-days-of-the-year living snowman, is happiest playing in the snow on Mount Beano.

DANDY TOWN
CROSSPATCH
NUTTY TOWN

BABY MINDER

If you need someone to look after your mini pranksters while you take care of business or just have a wander around Beanotown, the Baby Minder is here to help.

She understands children like nobody else, and is prepared for absolutely anything. She has gas masks, air freshener, and buckets of glue, glitter and poster paint at the ready.

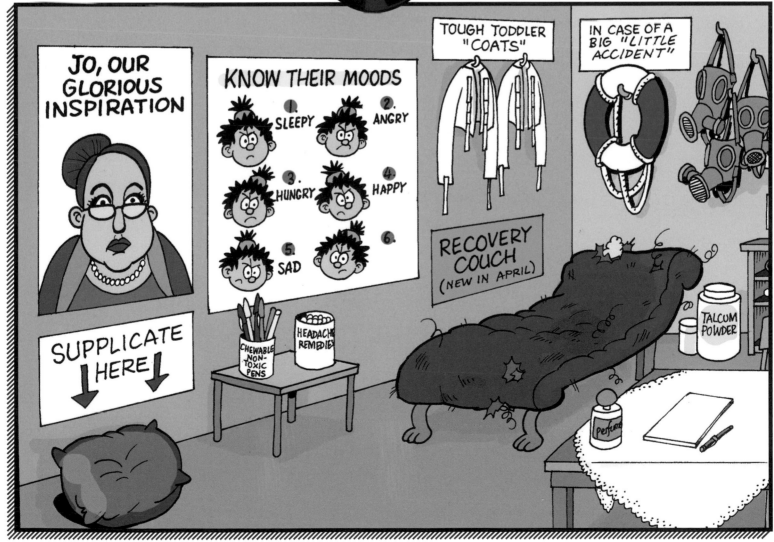

BEANOTOWN'S SECRETS

Everyone knows that Beanotown is filled with secrets. Some of them are simply pranks that have yet to be pulled. Others are life-changing truths about the past, present and future. Most of the residents have given up trying to understand them all.

THERE ARE ALWAYS MORE SECRETS TO DISCOVER. DENNIS AND HIS FRIENDS WERE ASTONISHED WHEN THEY STUMBLED ACROSS THE PLACE OF LOST THINGS IN BEANOTOWN WOODS.

PROFESSOR VON SCREWTOP

Rubi's dad is Professor von Screwtop, the best scientist in Beanotown. He's always experimenting with new and exciting ways of doing things. Sometimes his experiments go a little bit wrong, so it's important that he keeps them away from the prying eyes and twitching curtains of Beanotown's finest. His Top Secret Research Station contains all his coolest and craziest inventions.

DID YOU KNOW?
Among the professor's inventions are glow-in-the-dark slippers and a robot dog.

FACT FILE

BIRTHDAY: 5TH DECEMBER
ADDRESS: 112 MERCER STREET
JOB: RESEARCH SCIENTIST
LIKES: DISCOVERIES, SPACE, MATHS AND PHYSICS
DISLIKES: MAGPIES AND BLACK CATS
BIGGEST FEAR: RUNNING OUT OF QUESTIONS
BEST QUALITY: THE APPLIANCE OF SCIENCE IN DEFIANCE
TOP SKILLS: HE INVENTED A CHEESE TOASTIE MACHINE OUT OF AN OLD SUNBED AND A PAIR OF HAIR TONGS
FAVOURITE FOOD: HAIRY CHEESE TOASTIES

PERFECT PRANKS

Your guide to Beanotown is almost complete. Now you know a bit more about the place and the people, you'll understand why it's always a good idea to have a few pranks and dodges up your sleeve — just for emergencies, of course!

GLITTER TRICKER

1. WRITE A CARD.

2. PUT SOME GLITTER INTO A LITTLE POUCH OF TISSUE PAPER AND GLUE IT SHUT.

3. STICK THE POUCH INTO YOUR CARD, NEAR AN EDGE.

4. WAIT FOR THE CARD TO DRY.

5. WATCH WITH GLEE WHEN IT GETS OPENED. WHAT A MESS!

COOL AND CLEAN

1. PUT A TOOTHBRUSH INTO AN EMPTY COMPARTMENT OF AN ICE CUBE TRAY AND FILL THE TRAY WITH WATER.

2. FREEZE THE ICE CUBE TRAY.

3. WHEN THE WATER HAS FROZEN, REMOVE THE TOOTHBRUSH WITH THE ICE CUBE ATTACHED.

4. PUT IT IN THE TOOTHBRUSH HOLDER AND WAIT FOR THE CONFUSED REACTION!

MONSTER EYES

1. TAKE A TOILET PAPER TUBE AND CUT SOME EYES INTO IT.

2. TAPE A GLOW STICK INSIDE.

3. PUT THE TUBE INTO A BUSH OUTSIDE YOUR HOUSE TO MAKE YOUR PARENTS JUMP.

GLUG GLUG YUCK

DROP A FAKE FLY INTO SOMEONE'S GLASS OF WATER.

SPIDER SANDWICH

PLACE A FAKE CREEPY CRAWLY INSIDE YOUR FRIEND'S PACKED LUNCH BOX. SIMPLE AND EFFECTIVE.

WHERE <u>NOT</u> TO GO FOR HELP

If you're in trouble, or if you're confused or worried, there are a few simple rules to follow depending on who you are. If you are a grown-up who wants to complain about the state of Beanotown's pavements or ask questions about bin collections, you can skip this page. But if your problem is something really important, these are the places to avoid.

POLICE STATION

No. Sergeant Slipper won't help you. He'll just drone on with a whole list of boring questions and then ask you to fill out a form. Police Chief O'Reilly will call Bananaman, which often makes things worse. Just take a look at this snap of the police station and you'll see that they need your help more than you need theirs.

TOWN HALL

No, no, no. The only useful thing about the Town Hall is the clock tower on top of it. Everyone who works there is too busy sucking up to the Mayor and chasing parking fines to care about your problem.

MAYOR'S OFFICE

Wilbur Brown might help you if you're super important, super rich and enjoy giving your money away to greedy mayors. Otherwise, I'm afraid your luck is out. The only good reason to visit his office is to speak to his personal assistant, Sandra Menace, and ask her where to find her son.

WHERE TO GO FOR HELP

DENNIS'S DEN

Drum roll please… all fair-minded top pranksters will find help if they head to Dennis's den. Rubi, JJ and Pieface will all be happy to lend a hand, and Gnasher will do anything for you if you take along a string of sausages.

BEANOTOWN QUIZ

Have you been paying attention or have you been too busy making paper aeroplanes at the back of the class? Complete this quiz to see how much you have learned about Beanotown – and find out which resident would be your perfect playmate!

1. WHERE IS DENNIS'S DEN?

2. WHO BUILT THE VERY FIRST BEANOTOWN?

3. WHICH FAMILY LIVES IN A HOUSE CALLED "TRANQUILITY"?

4. HOW TALL IS MOUNT BEANO?

5. WHO DOES ERIC WIMP HAVE A CRUSH ON?

6. WHERE ARE THE ANNUAL SAND SCULPTURE CHAMPIONSHIPS HELD?

7. HOW MANY PUPPIES DOES GNASHER HAVE?

8. WHO IS THE BEANOTOWN LIBRARIAN?

9. WHAT DOES SMIRK STAND FOR?

10. WHO PROTECTS THE BOOK OF BEANOTOWN SECRETS?

11. WHAT IS THE RELATIONSHIP BETWEEN DENNIS AND MINNIE?

12. WHERE MIGHT YOU FIND A VOLCANO, A GIANT DOG AND A WORRYING NUMBER OF DINOSAURS?

13. WHICH SPORTY DRUMMER RIDES A BMX?

14. HOW MANY TIMES HAS BASH STREET SCHOOL BEEN REBUILT?

15. WHO LIVES IN BUNKERTON CASTLE?

16. WHICH ANIMAL BOASTS THE MOST ESCAPES FROM BEANOTOWN ZOO?

17. WHO INVENTED THE SQUELCHY THINGS?

18. WHERE IS THE SKATE PARK?

19. WHO HAS A BED PERMANENTLY RESERVED IN BEANOTOWN HOSPITAL?

20. WHICH ANIMAL PROVIDED THE RED WOOL FOR DENNIS'S JUMPER?

Turn the page for the answers!

ANSWERS

1. BEANOTOWN WOODS
2. VIKINGS
3. THE BROWN FAMILY
4. 1,938 METRES
5. FIONA THE NEWSREADER
6. BEANOTOWN-ON-SEA
7. SIX
8. BETTY'S YETI'S UNCLE
9. SECRET MINISTRY OF INTELLIGENT ROTTERS KOMITTEE.
10. THE GHOST LIBRARIAN
11. THEY ARE COUSINS
12. DUCK ISLAND
13. JJ
14. 24
15. LORD SNOOTY
16. ELLIS THE ELEPHANT
17. PROFESSOR CRACKPOTT
18. IN FRONT OF BASH STREET SCHOOL
19. CALAMITY JAMES
20. RODNEY THE RAM

HOW DID YOU DO?

1-6 You can learn the facts another time – you live for the action! Head for the skate park with Dennis and you'll have a ton of fun.

7-11 You know just enough to get by, as long as you have a few tricks up your sleeve. You'll learn even more while you're hanging out with Roger.

12-16 Awesome score, well done! You're smart, quick and the perfect friend for Minnie.

17-20 Amazeballs! You're a Beanotown expert. You'll love hanging out with Rubi and dreaming up some new inventions.